FIGMENT 2

THE LEGACY OF IMAGINATION: VOLUME 5

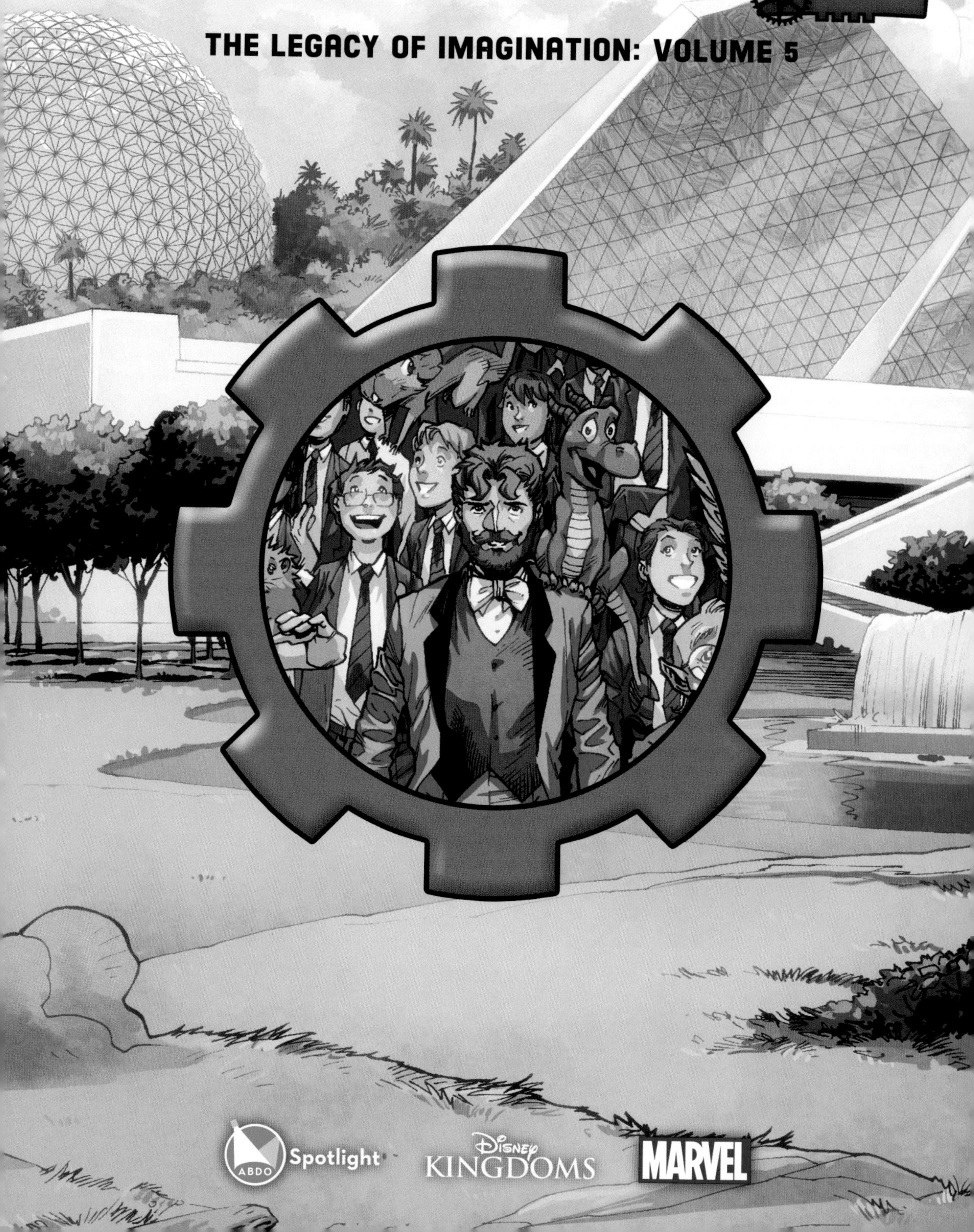

ABDO Spotlight
Disney Kingdoms
MARVEL

ABDOPUBLISHING.COM

Reinforced library bound edition published in 2017 by Spotlight,
a division of ABDO, PO Box 398166, Minneapolis, Minnesota 55439.
Spotlight produces high-quality reinforced library bound editions for
schools and libraries. Published by agreement with Marvel Characters, Inc.

Printed in the United States of America, North Mankato, Minnesota.
092016
012017

THIS BOOK CONTAINS
RECYCLED MATERIALS

marvelkids.com
© 2016 MARVEL

Elements based on Figment © Disney.

PUBLISHER'S CATALOGING IN PUBLICATION DATA

Names: Zub, Jim, author. | Bachs, Ramon ; Beaulieu, Jean-Francois, illustrators.
Title: Figment 2 : The Legacy of Imagination / writer: Jim Zub ; art: Ramon Bachs
  ; Jean-Francois Beaulieu.
Description: Reinforced library bound edition. | Minneapolis, Minnesota : Spotlight,
  2017. | Series: Disney Kingdoms : Figment Set 2
Summary: After flying through a portal, Dreamfinder and Figment find themselves
  in the 21st century at the new Academy, but when a demonstration goes
  wrong, Dreamfinder transforms into the Doubtfinder, leaving Figment and
  Capri to free Dreamfinder before doubt can take over the world.
Identifiers: LCCN 2016941716 | ISBN 9781614795810 (volume 1) | ISBN
  9781614795827 (volume 2) | ISBN 9781614795834 (volume 3) | ISBN
  9781614795841 (volume 4) | ISBN 9781614795858 (volume 5)
Subjects: LCSH: Disney (Fictitious characters)--Juvenile fiction. | Adventure and
  adventurers--Juvenile fiction. | Comic books, strips, etc.--Juvenile fiction. |
  Graphic novels--Juvenile fiction.
Classification: DDC 741.5--dc23
LC record available at https://lccn.loc.gov/2016941716

Spotlight

A Division of ABDO
abdopublishing.com

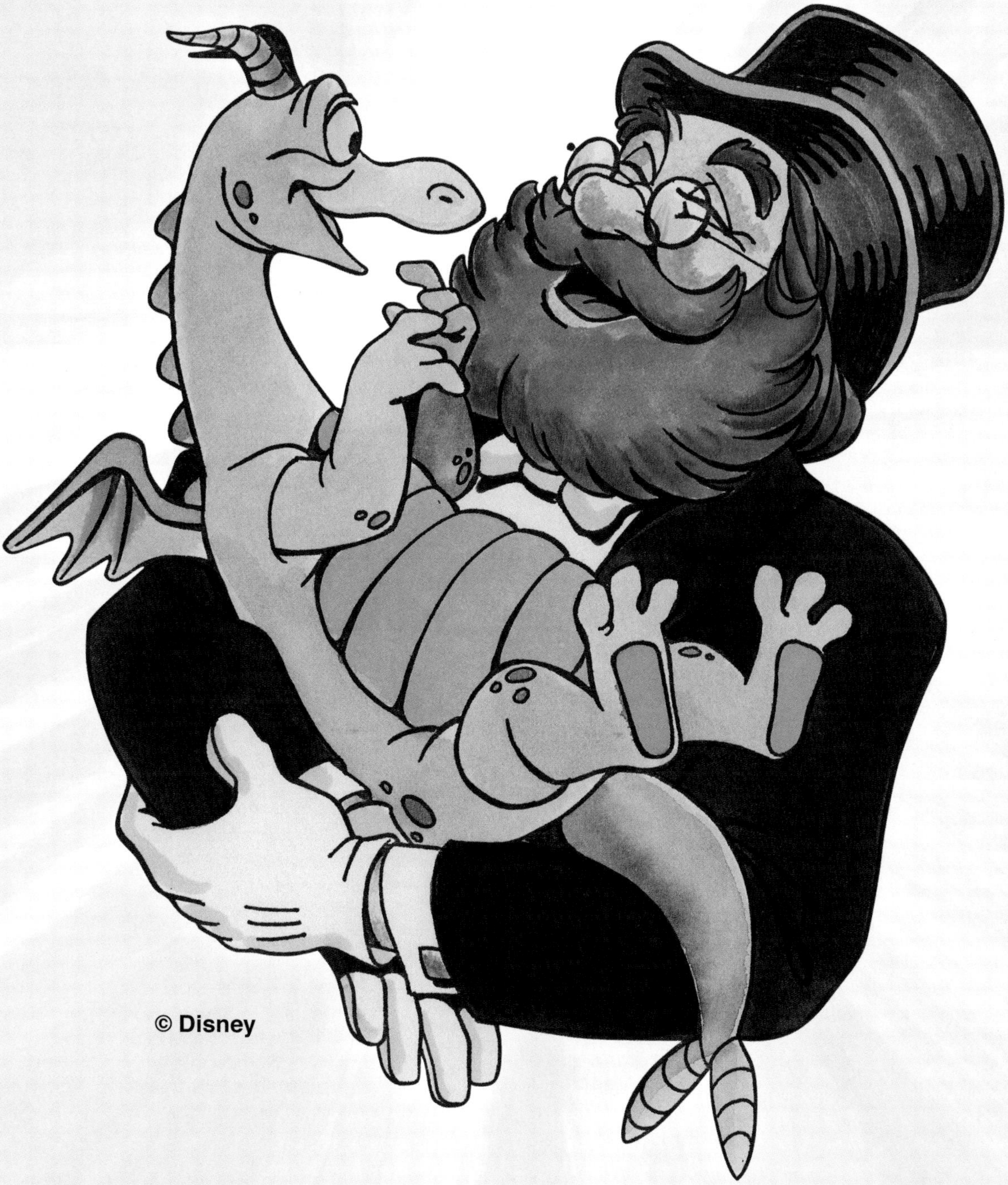

Early Figment and Dreamfinder character designs for the Journey Into Imagination ride by X Atencio

Artwork courtesy of Walt Disney Imagineering Art Collection

Times change. **Dreamfinder** and **Figment** found that out the hard way when they traveled from 1910 London to 21st-century Florida. Unsure of himself in this strange new world, Dreamfinder's imagination demonstration at the modern-day Academy Scientifica-Lucidus, arranged by his professor friend **Fye** even at the protest of the school's **Chairman Auckley**, went so poorly that his self-doubt fueled a nightmarish creature that took over his mind to create the **Doubtfinder**.

The Doubtfinder turned the creative people at the Academy into mindless slaves. Unaffected, Figment fled the Academy in search of help, which he found in **Capricious Harmony**, the great-great-great-grandniece of Dreamfinder. They returned to confront the Doubt, and with the Mesmonic Converter Helmet in hand, Capri summoned a figment of her own imagination – **Spark** – before opening a portal into Doubtfinder's shadowy mindscape.

The trio of dream adventurers encountered numerous challenges, but were able to break Dreamfinder free of his doubt and return to the real world...only to find the Doubt no longer needed Dreamfinder's body and had taken on a monstrous form of its own!

Dreamfinder   **Figment**   **Chairman Auckley**   **Fye**

DOUBT **Dreamfinder**   **Capri**   **Spark**

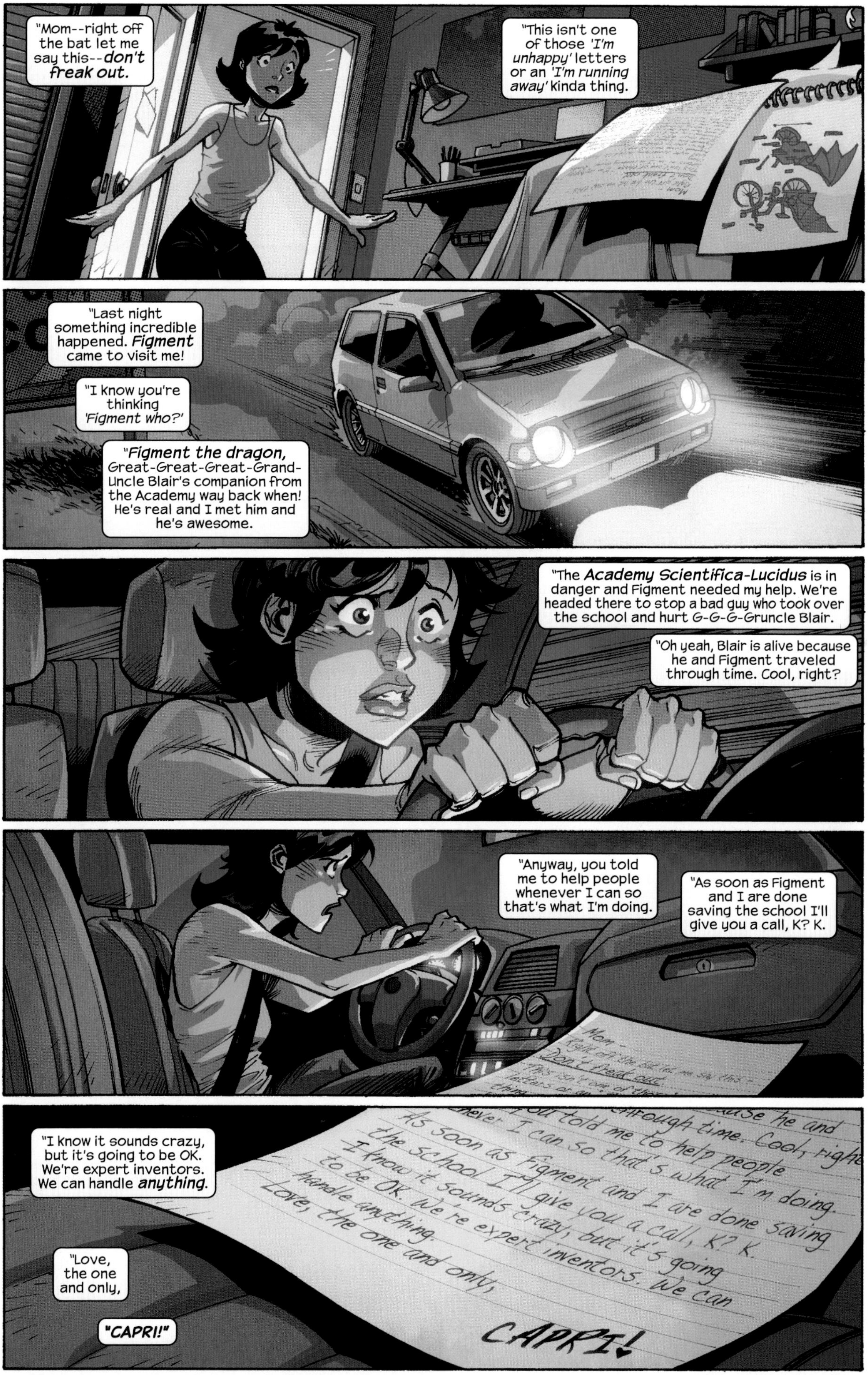
"Mom--right off the bat let me say this--*don't freak out.*
"This isn't one of those *'I'm unhappy'* letters or an *'I'm running away'* kinda thing.
"Last night something incredible happened. ***Figment*** came to visit me!
"I know you're thinking *'Figment who?'*
"***Figment the dragon,*** Great-Great-Great-Grand-Uncle Blair's companion from the Academy way back when! He's real and I met him and he's awesome.
"The ***Academy Scientifica-Lucidus*** is in danger and Figment needed my help. We're headed there to stop a bad guy who took over the school and hurt G-G-G-Gruncle Blair.
"Oh yeah, Blair is alive because he and Figment traveled through time. Cool, right?
"Anyway, you told me to help people whenever I can so that's what I'm doing.
"As soon as Figment and I are done saving the school I'll give you a call, K? K.
"I know it sounds crazy, but it's going to be OK. We're expert inventors. We can handle ***anything.***
"Love, the one and only,
"CAPRI!"

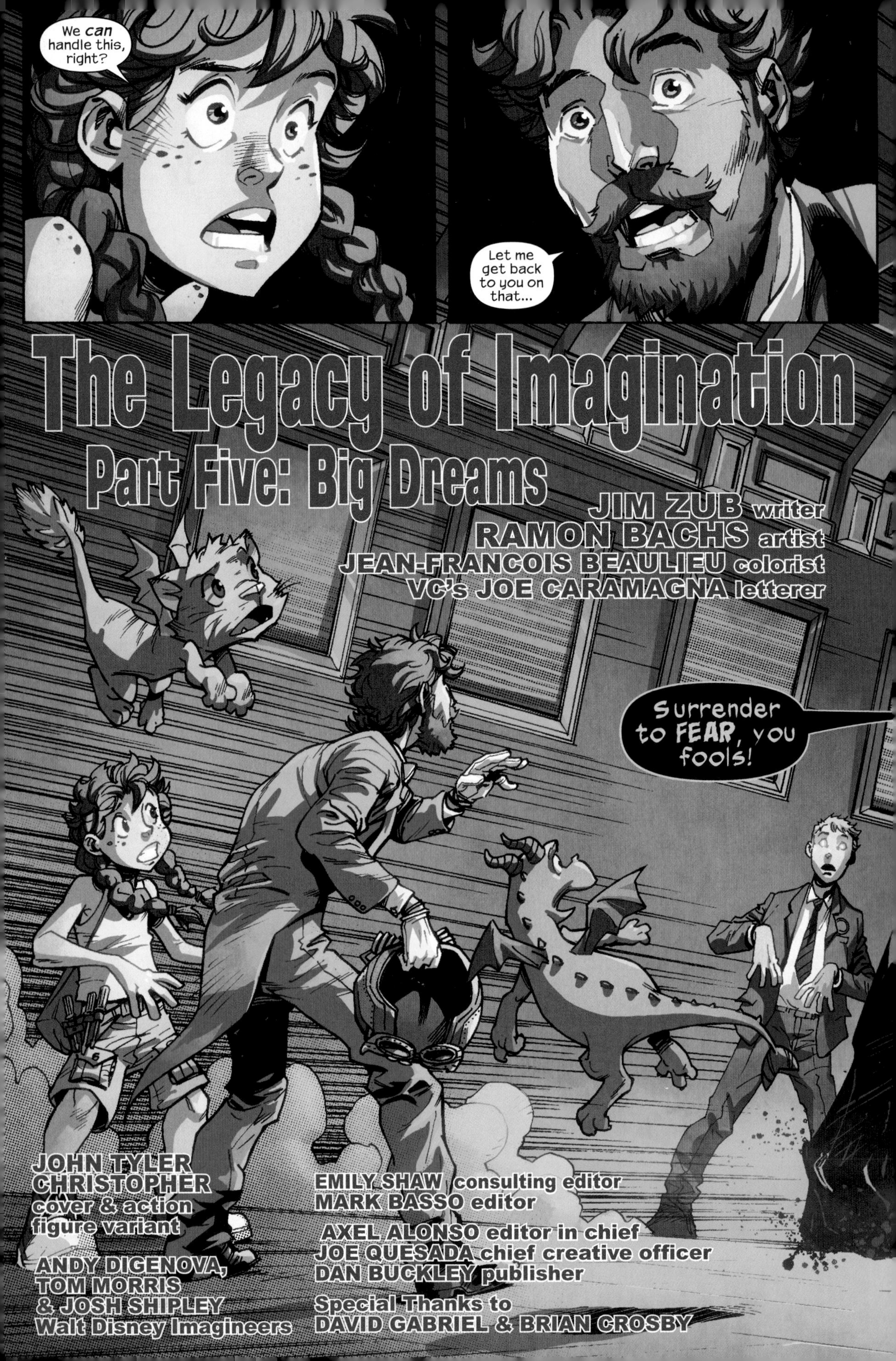

We *can* handle this, right?
Let me get back to you on that...
The Legacy of Imagination
Part Five: Big Dreams
JIM ZUB writer
RAMON BACHS artist
JEAN-FRANCOIS BEAULIEU colorist
VC's JOE CARAMAGNA letterer
Surrender to **FEAR**, you fools!
JOHN TYLER CHRISTOPHER cover & action figure variant
ANDY DIGENOVA, TOM MORRIS & JOSH SHIPLEY Walt Disney Imagineers
EMILY SHAW consulting editor
MARK BASSO editor
AXEL ALONSO editor in chief
JOE QUESADA chief creative officer
DAN BUCKLEY publisher
Special Thanks to DAVID GABRIEL & BRIAN CROSBY

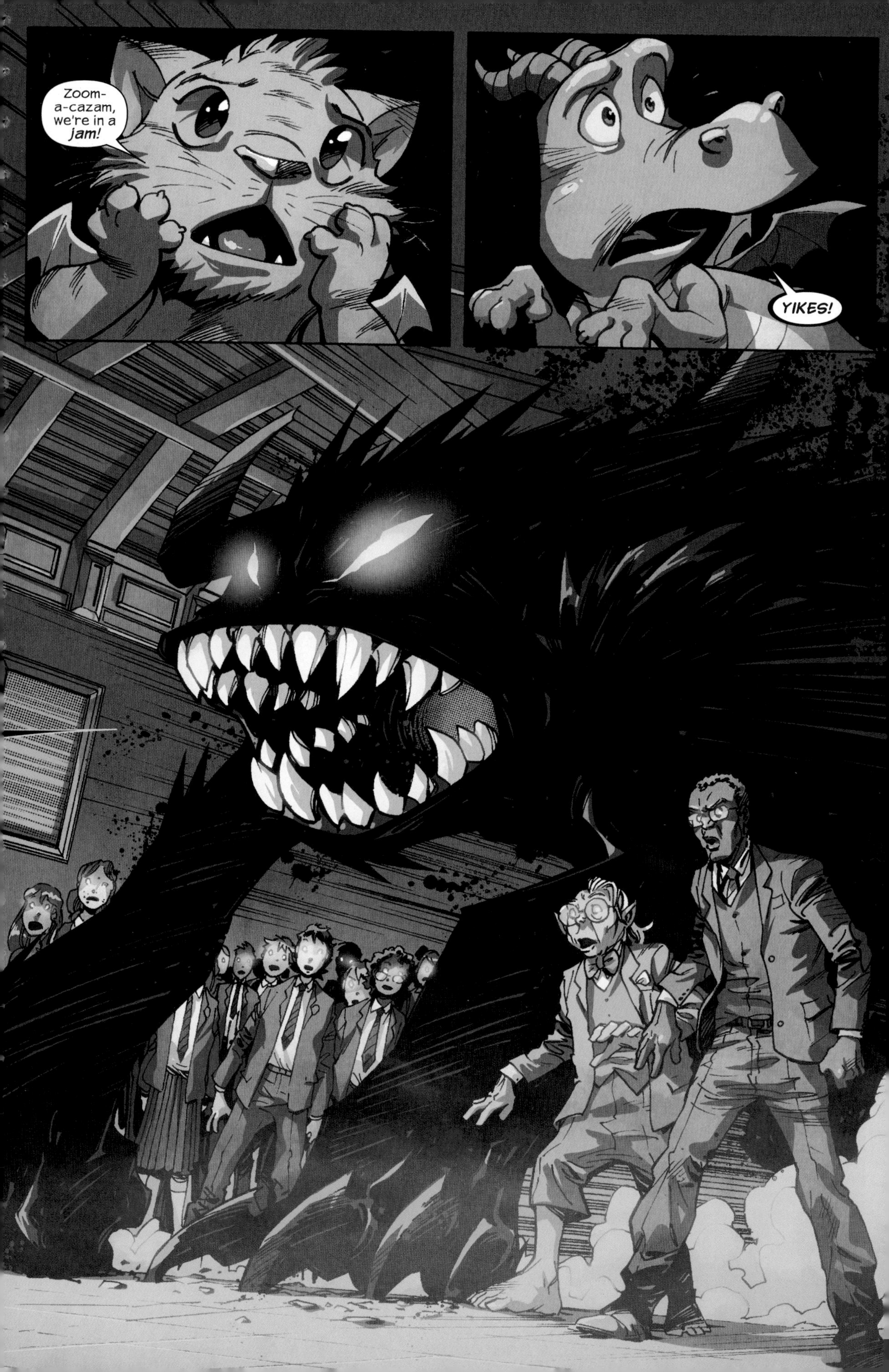
Zoom-
a-cazam,
we're in a
jam!
YIKES!

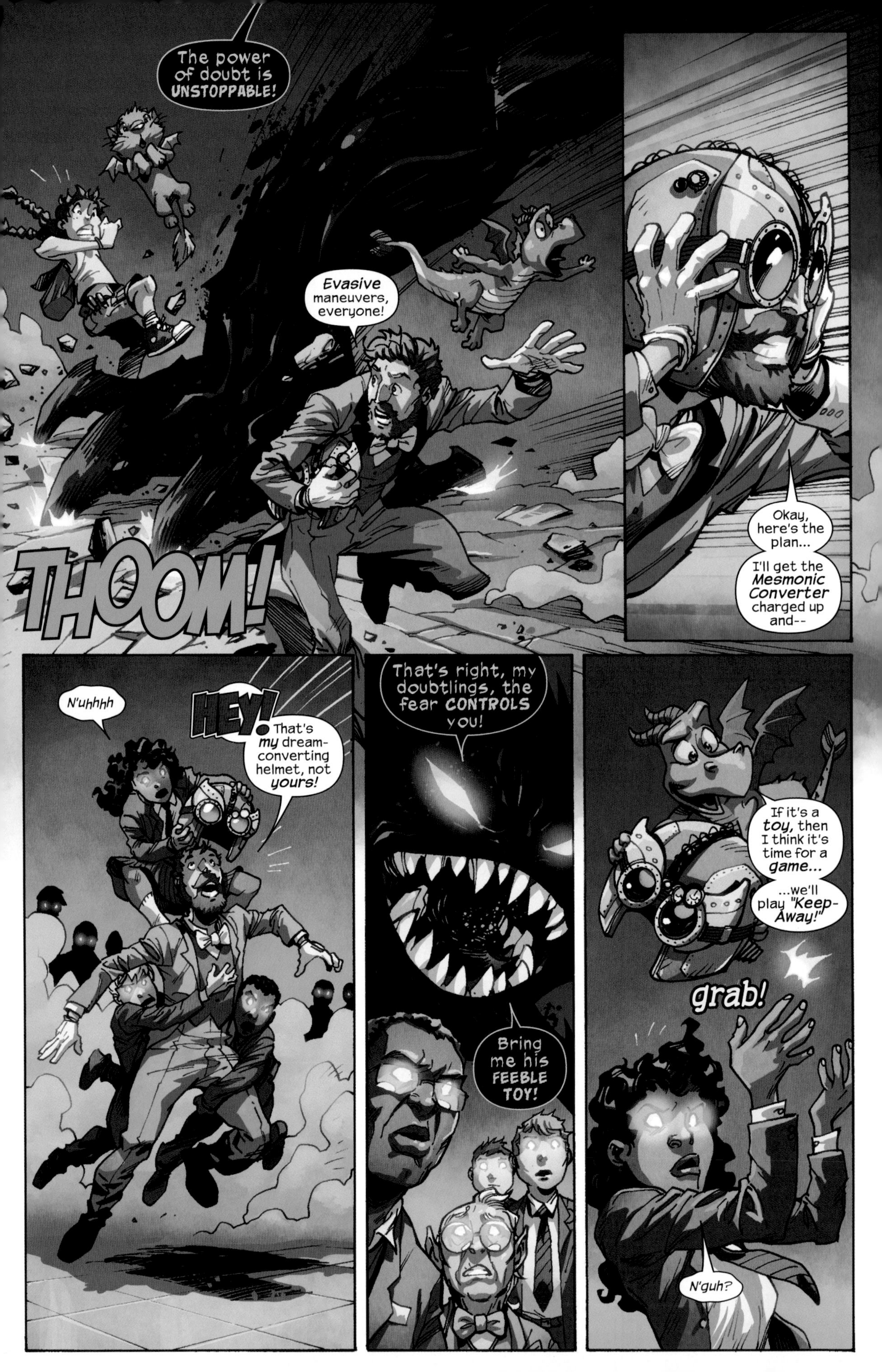
The power of doubt is UNSTOPPABLE!
Evasive maneuvers, everyone!
THOOM!
Okay, here's the plan...
I'll get the Mesmonic Converter charged up and--
N'uhhhh
HEY!
That's my dream-converting helmet, not yours!
That's right, my doubtlings, the fear CONTROLS you!
Bring me his FEEBLE TOY!
If it's a toy, then I think it's time for a game...
...we'll play "Keep-Away!"
grab!
N'guh?

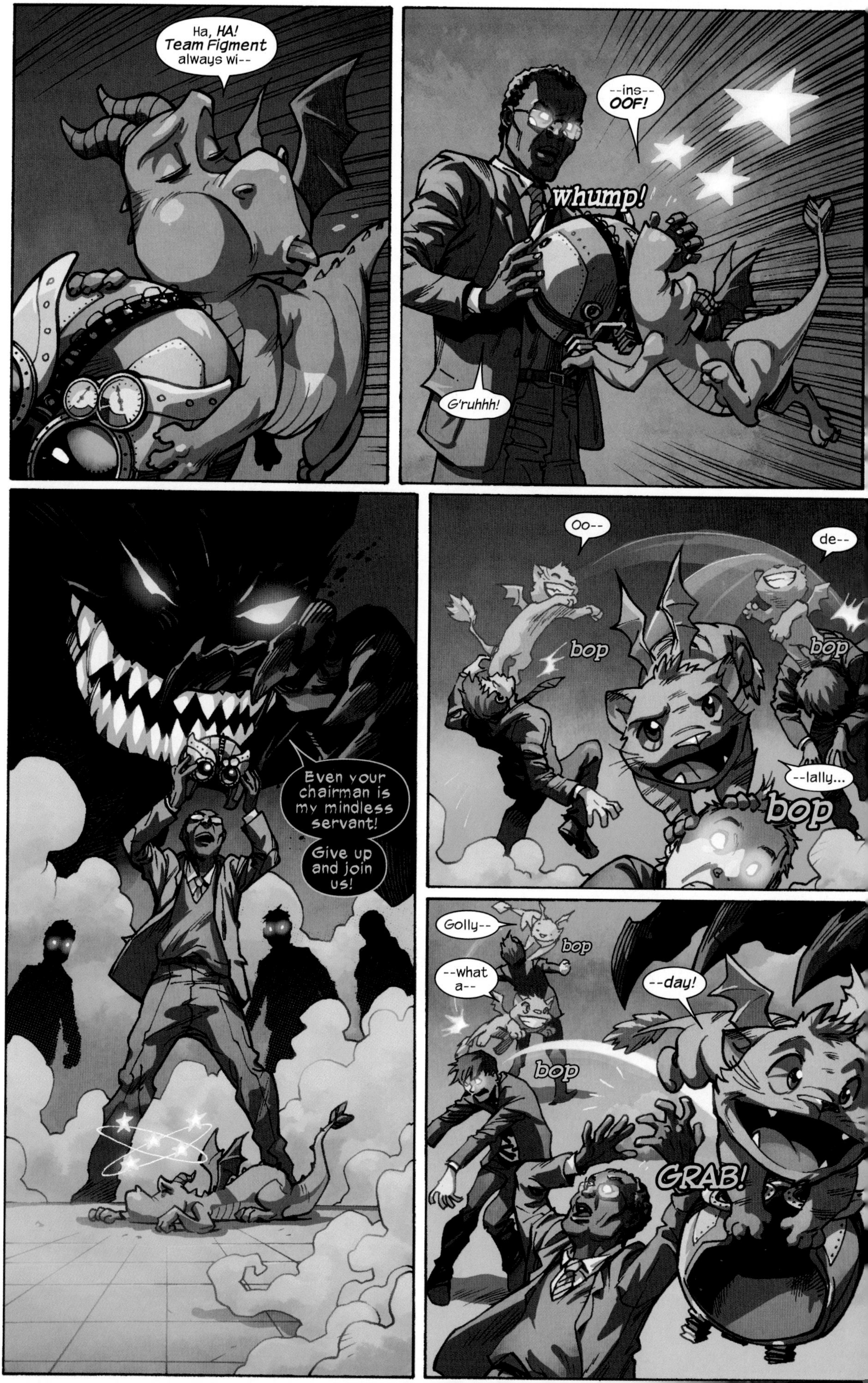
Ha, HA! Team Figment always wi--
--ins-- OOF!
Whump!
G'ruhhh!
Even your chairman is my mindless servant!
Give up and join us!
Oo--
bop
de--
bop
--lally...
bop
Golly--
bop
--what a--
--day!
bop
GRAB!

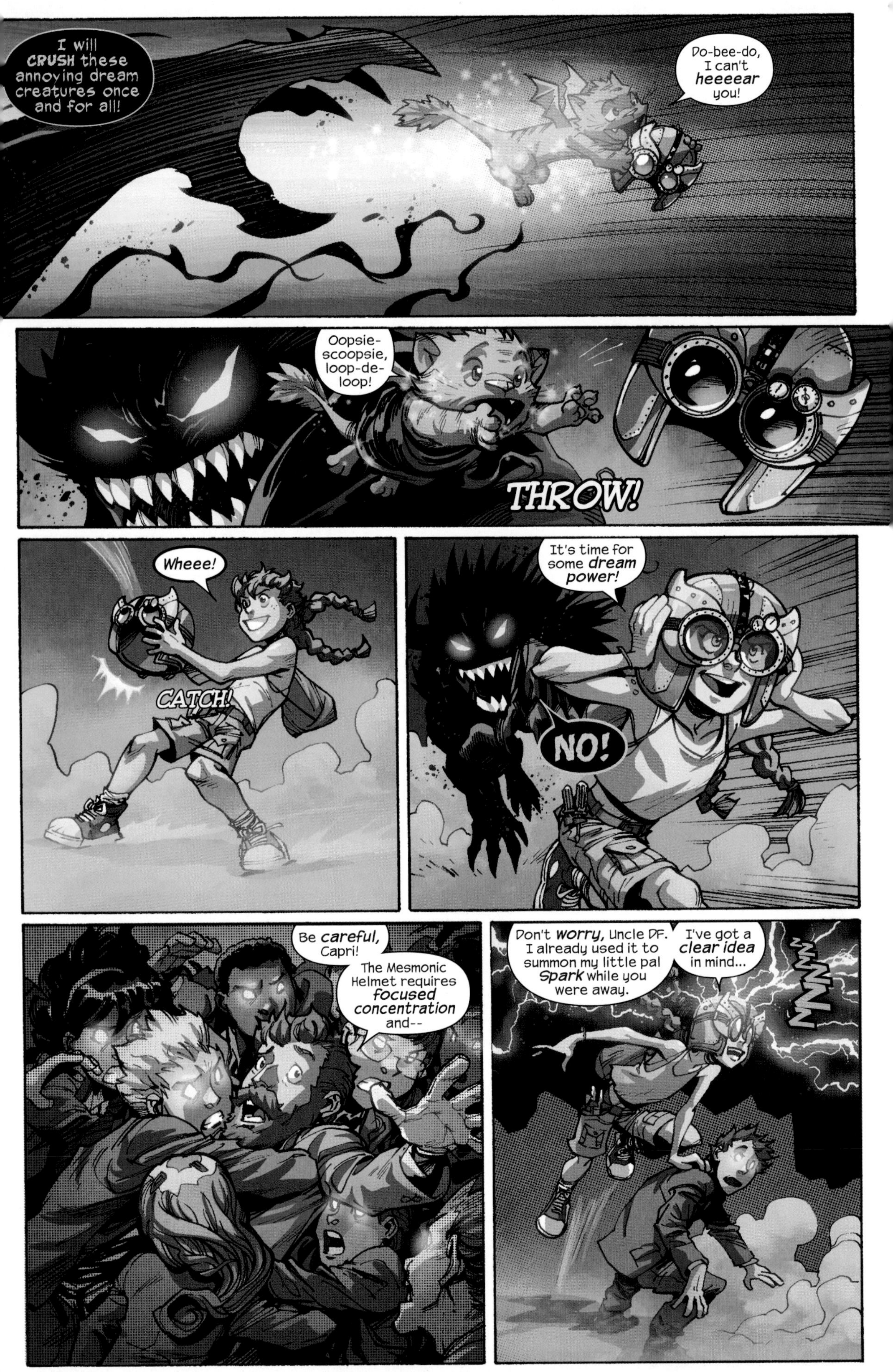

I will CRUSH these annoying dream creatures once and for all!
Do-bee-do, I can't heeeear you!
Oopsie-scoopsie, loop-de-loop!
THROW!
Wheee!
CATCH!
It's time for some dream power!
NO!
Be careful, Capri!
The Mesmonic Helmet requires focused concentration and--
Don't worry, Uncle DF. I already used it to summon my little pal Spark while you were away.
I've got a clear idea in mind...
MMMMM

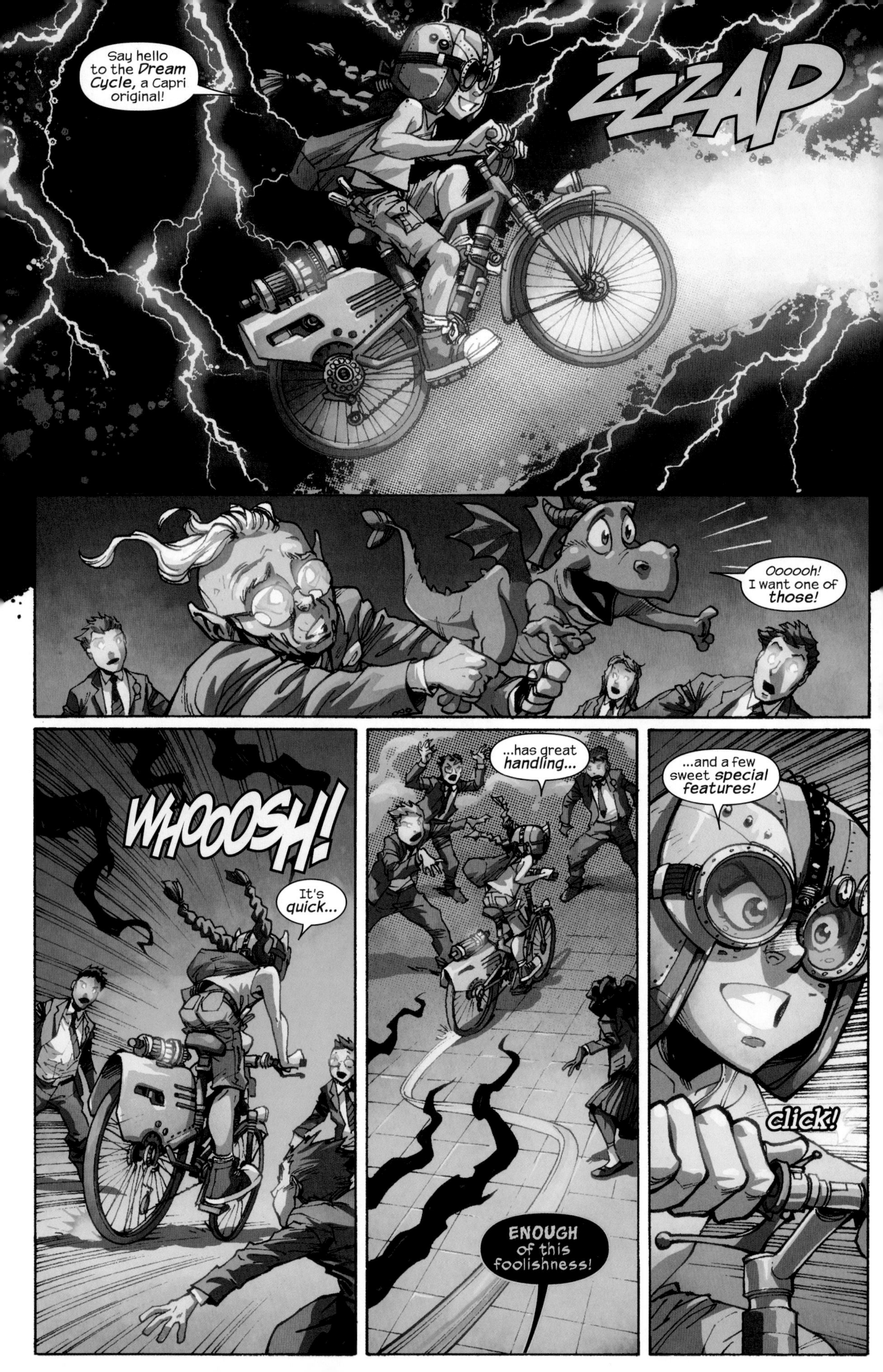
Say hello to the *Dream Cycle,* a Capri original!
ZZZAP
Oooooh! I want one of *those!*
WHOOOSH!
It's *quick...*
...has great *handling...*
ENOUGH of this foolishness!
...and a few sweet *special features!*
click!

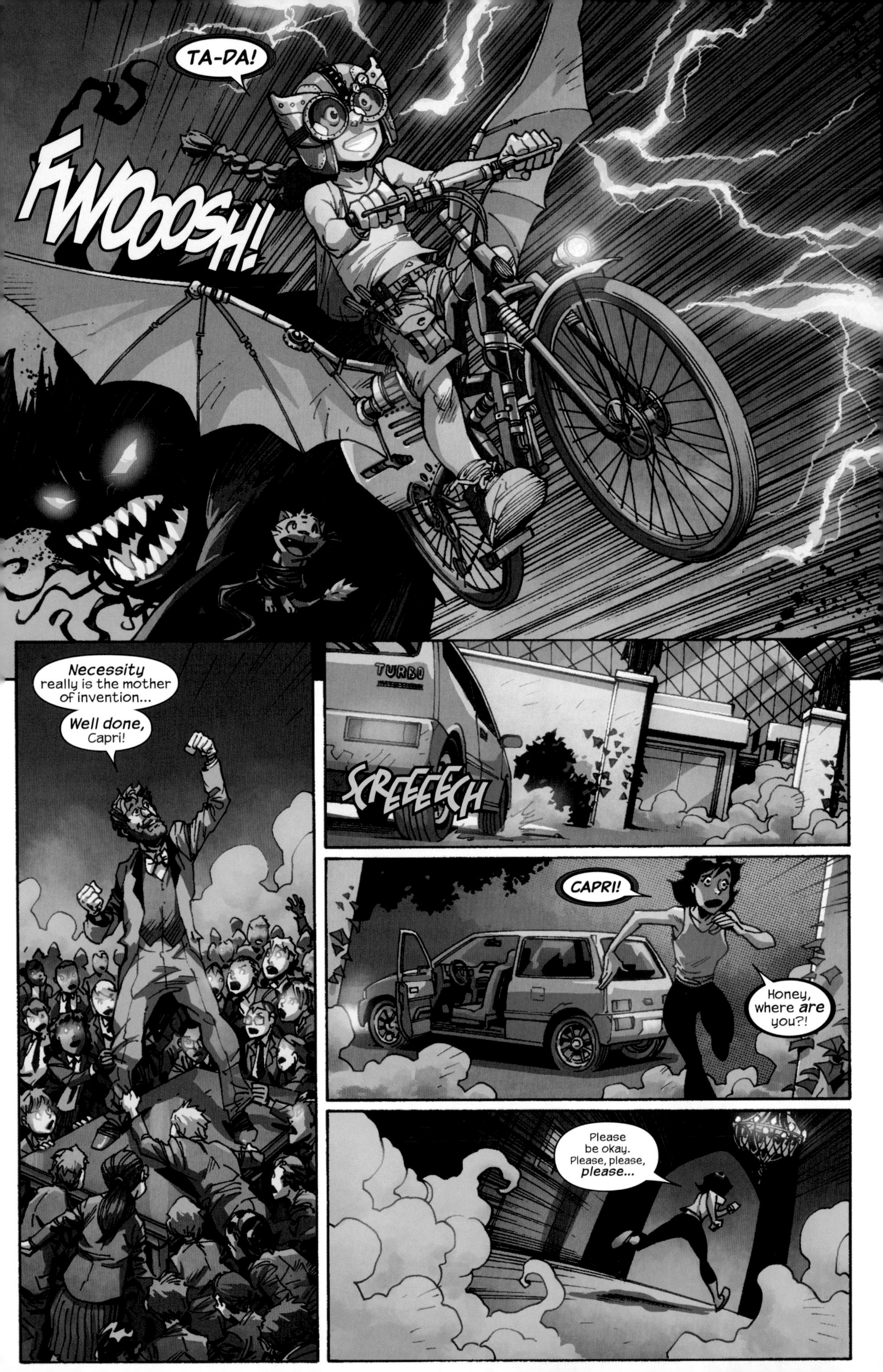
TA-DA!
FWOOOSH!
Necessity really is the mother of invention...
Well done, Capri!
TURBO
SCREEEECH
CAPRI!
Honey, where are you?!
Please be okay. Please, please, please...

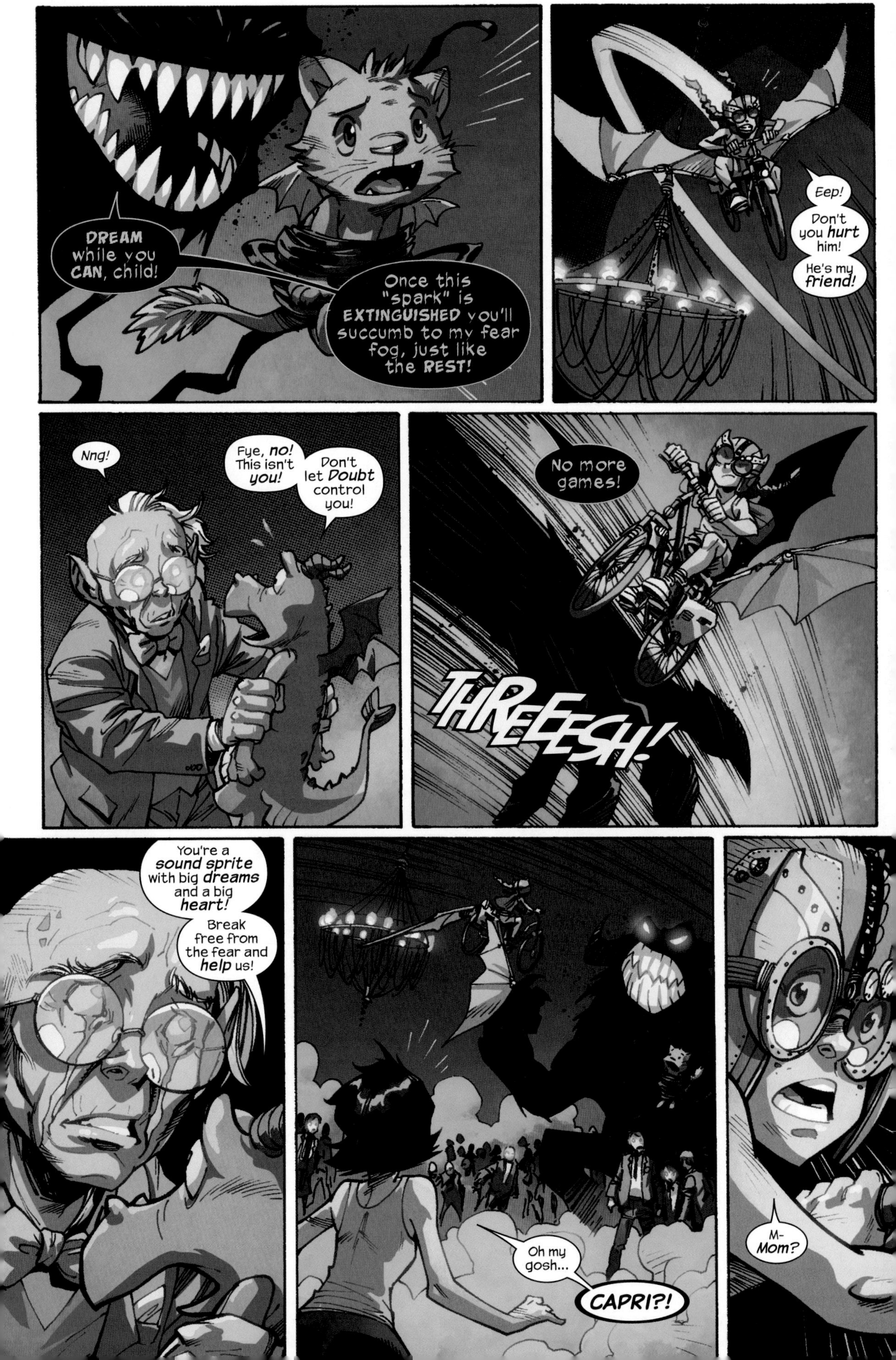
DREAM while you CAN, child!
Once this "spark" is EXTINGUISHED you'll succumb to my fear fog, just like the REST!
Eep!
Don't you hurt him!
He's my friend!
Nng!
Fye, no! This isn't you!
Don't let Doubt control you!
No more games!
THREEEESH!
You're a sound sprite with big dreams and a big heart!
Break free from the fear and help us!
Oh my gosh...
CAPRI?!
M-Mom?

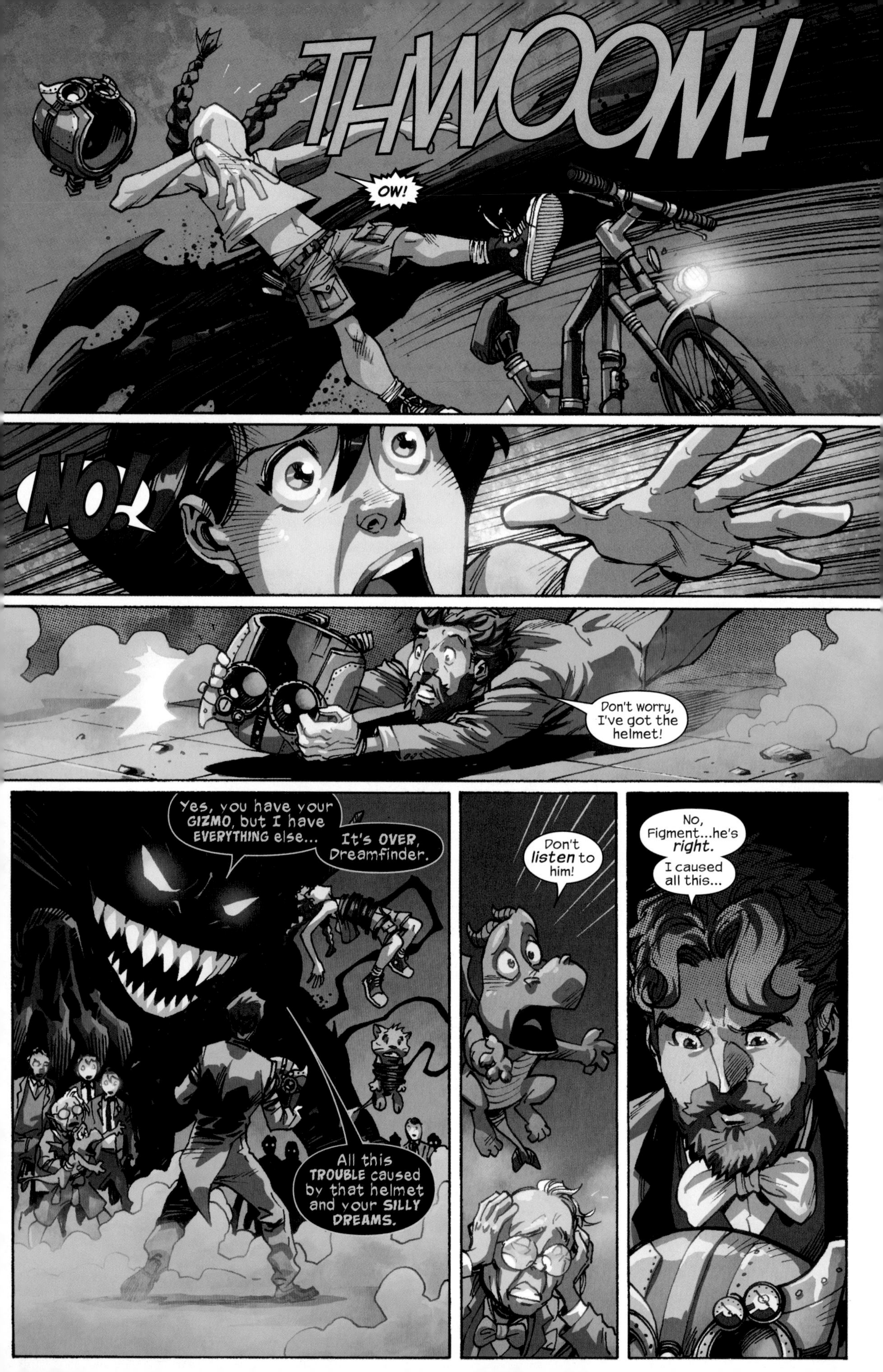
THWOOM!
OW!
NO!
Don't worry, I've got the helmet!
Yes, you have your GIZMO, but I have EVERYTHING else...
It's OVER, Dreamfinder.
All this TROUBLE caused by that helmet and your SILLY DREAMS.
Don't listen to him!
No, Figment...he's right.
I caused all this...

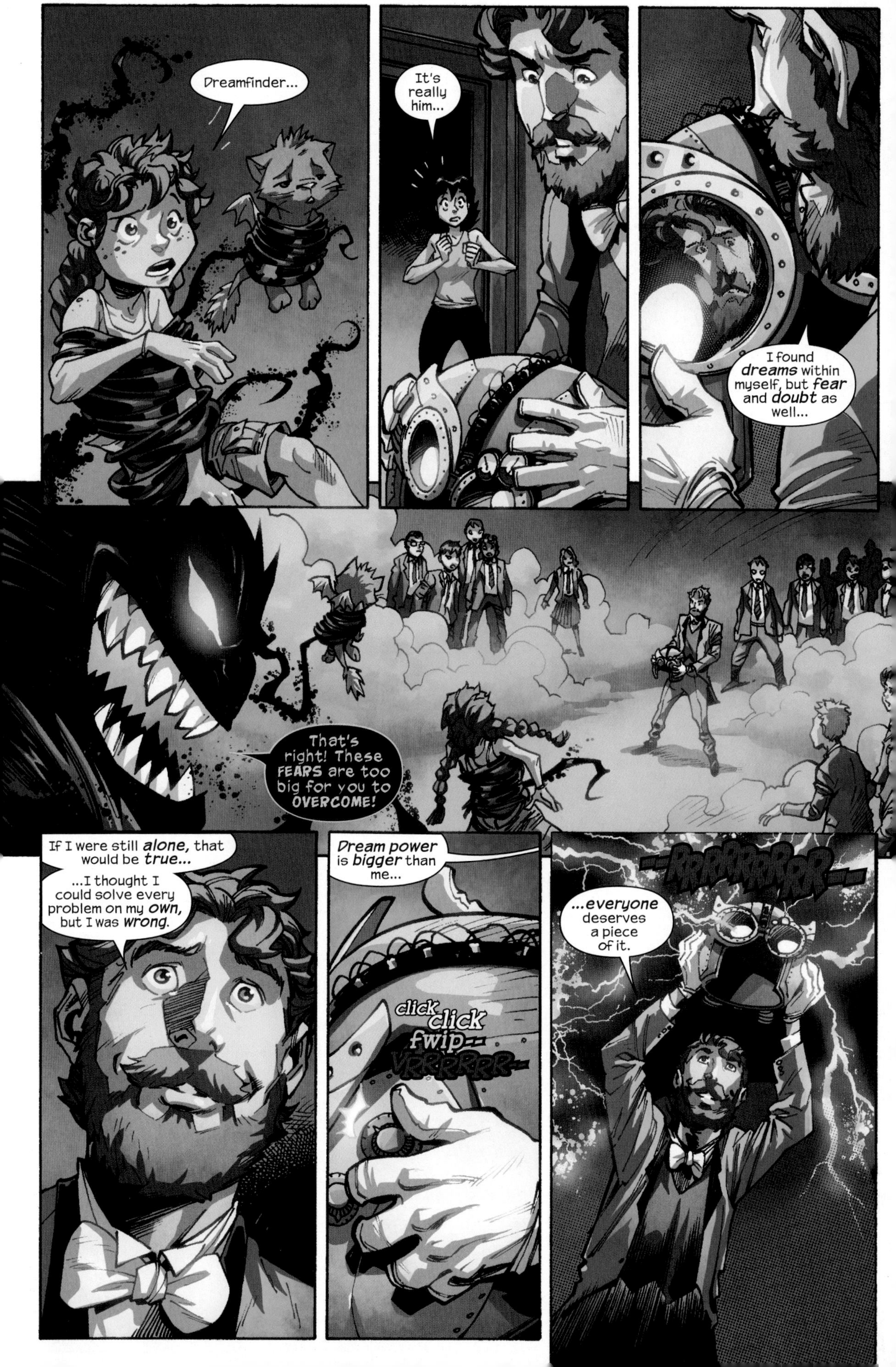
Dreamfinder...
It's really him...
I found dreams within myself, but fear and doubt as well...
That's right! These FEARS are too big for you to OVERCOME!
If I were still alone, that would be true...
...I thought I could solve every problem on my own, but I was wrong.
Dream power is bigger than me...
click click fwip--
VRRRRRR--
--RRRRRRRRRR--
...everyone deserves a piece of it.

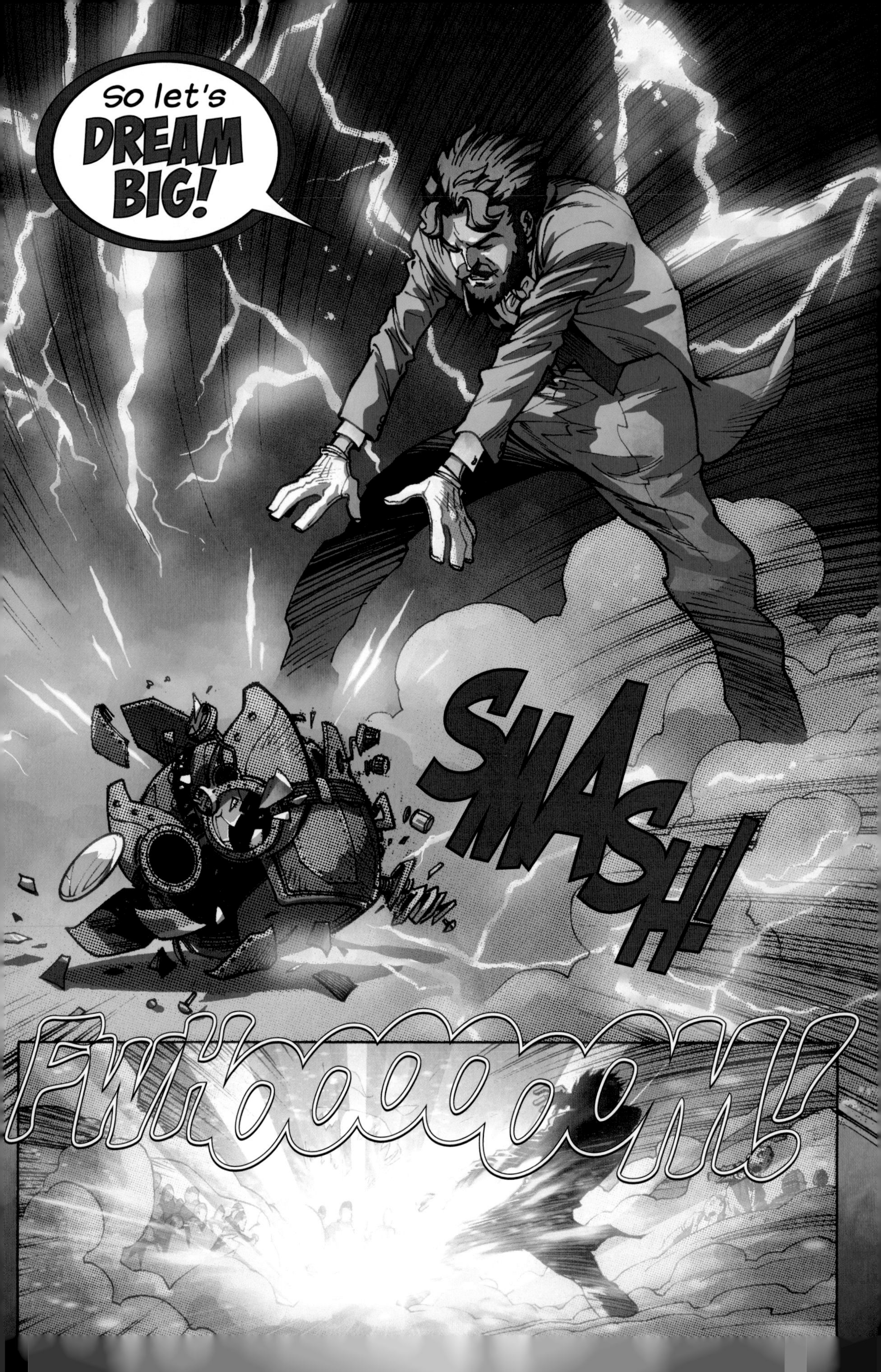
So let's DREAM BIG!
SMASH!
FWHOOOOOOM!

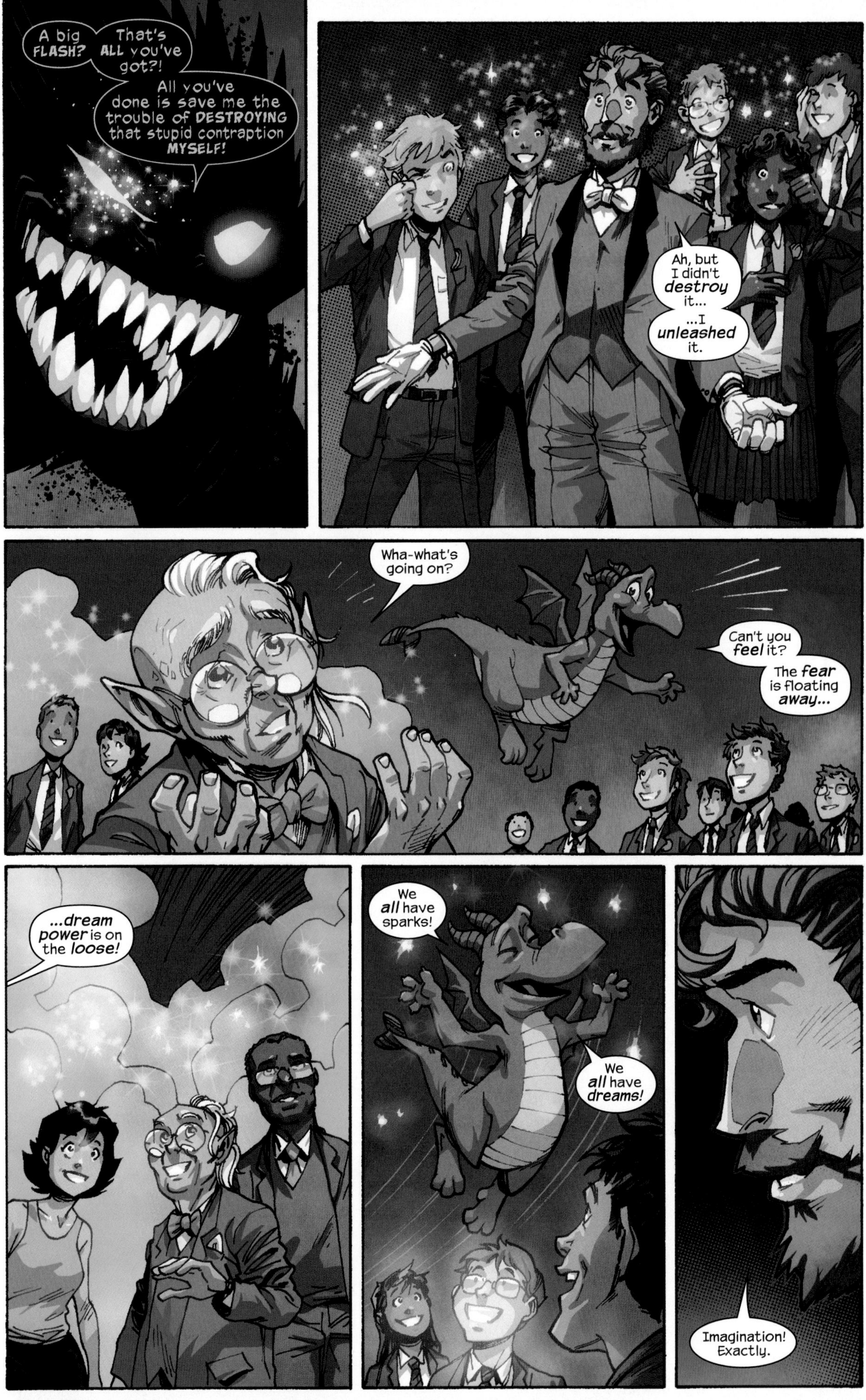

A big FLASH?
That's ALL you've got?!
All you've done is save me the trouble of DESTROYING that stupid contraption MYSELF!
Ah, but I didn't destroy it...
...I unleashed it.
Wha-what's going on?
Can't you feel it?
The fear is floating away...
...dream power is on the loose!
We all have sparks!
We all have dreams!
Imagination! Exactly.

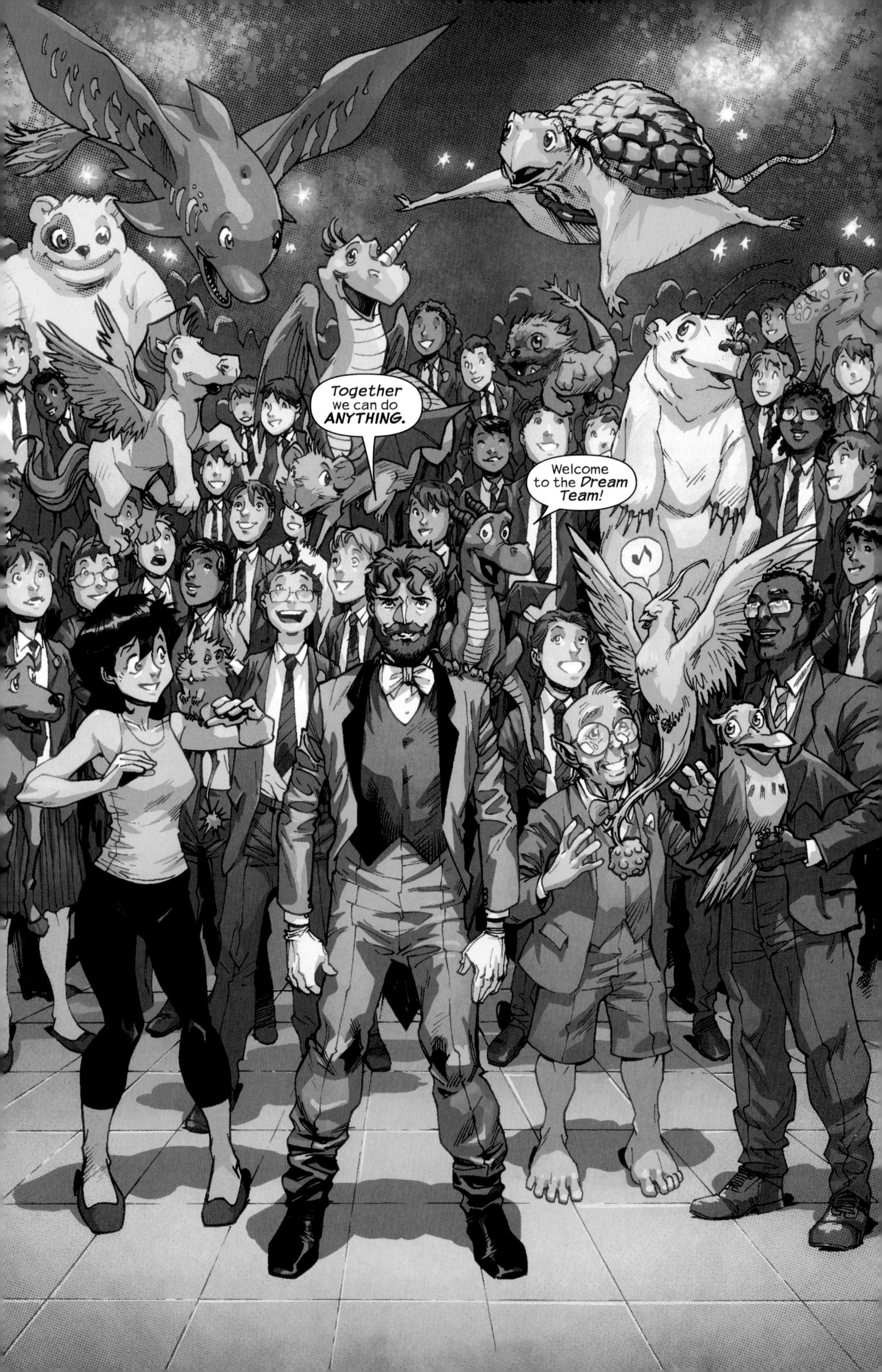
Together we can do ANYTHING.
Welcome to the Dream Team!

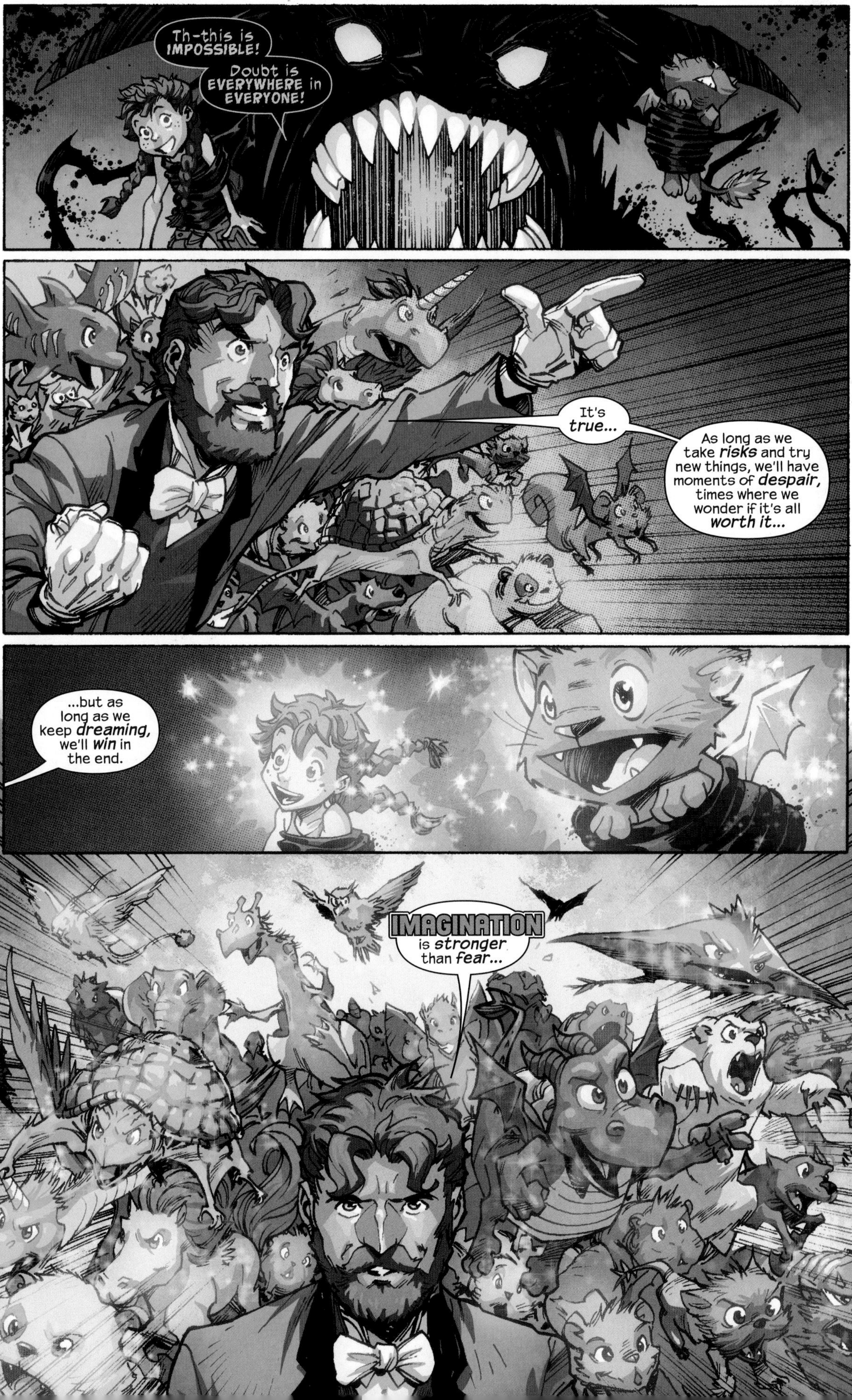
Th-this is IMPOSSIBLE!
Doubt is EVERYWHERE in EVERYONE!
It's true...
As long as we take risks and try new things, we'll have moments of despair, times where we wonder if it's all worth it...
...but as long as we keep dreaming, we'll win in the end.
IMAGINATION is stronger than fear...

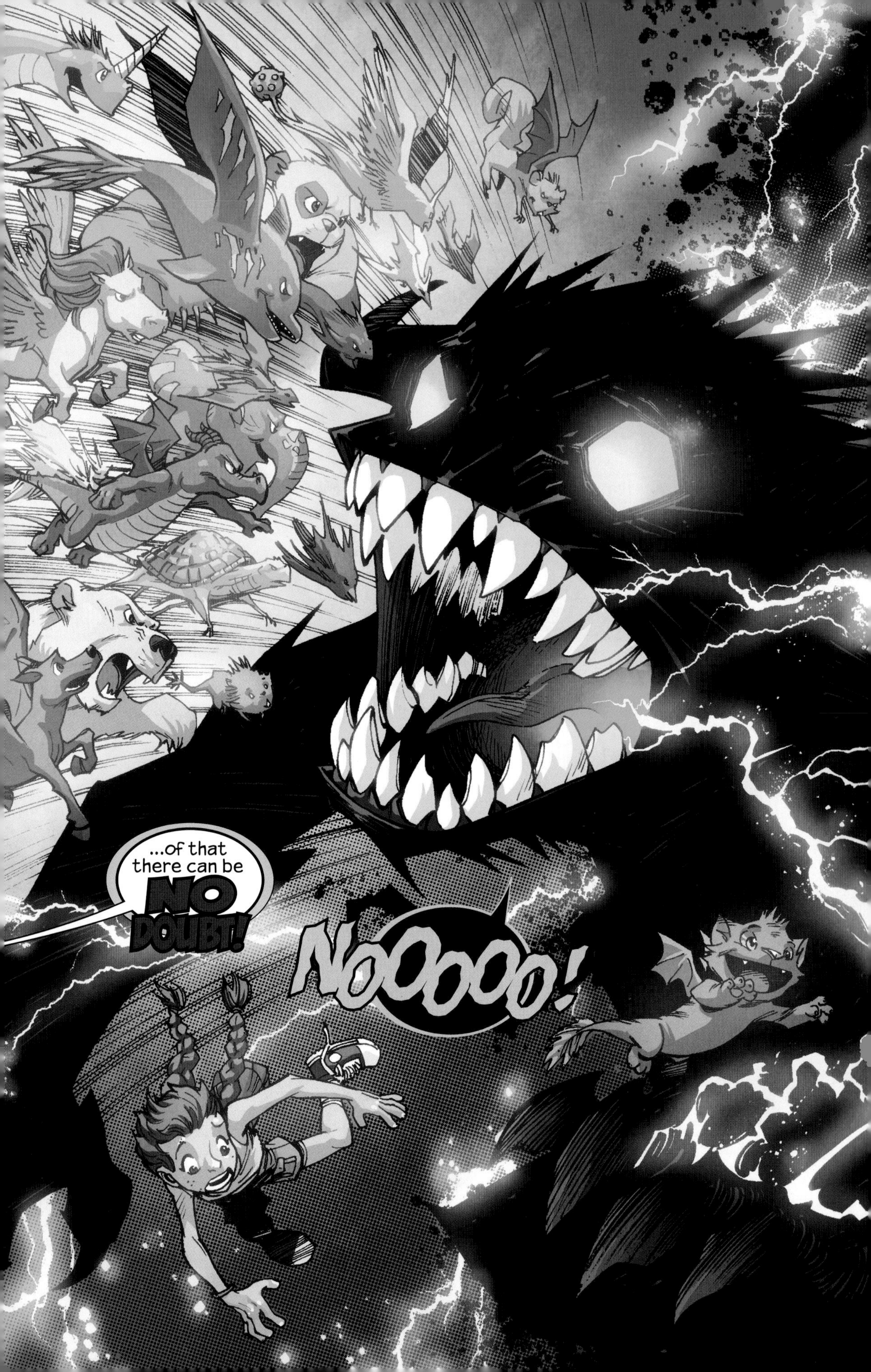
...of that there can be NO DOUBT!
NOOOOO!

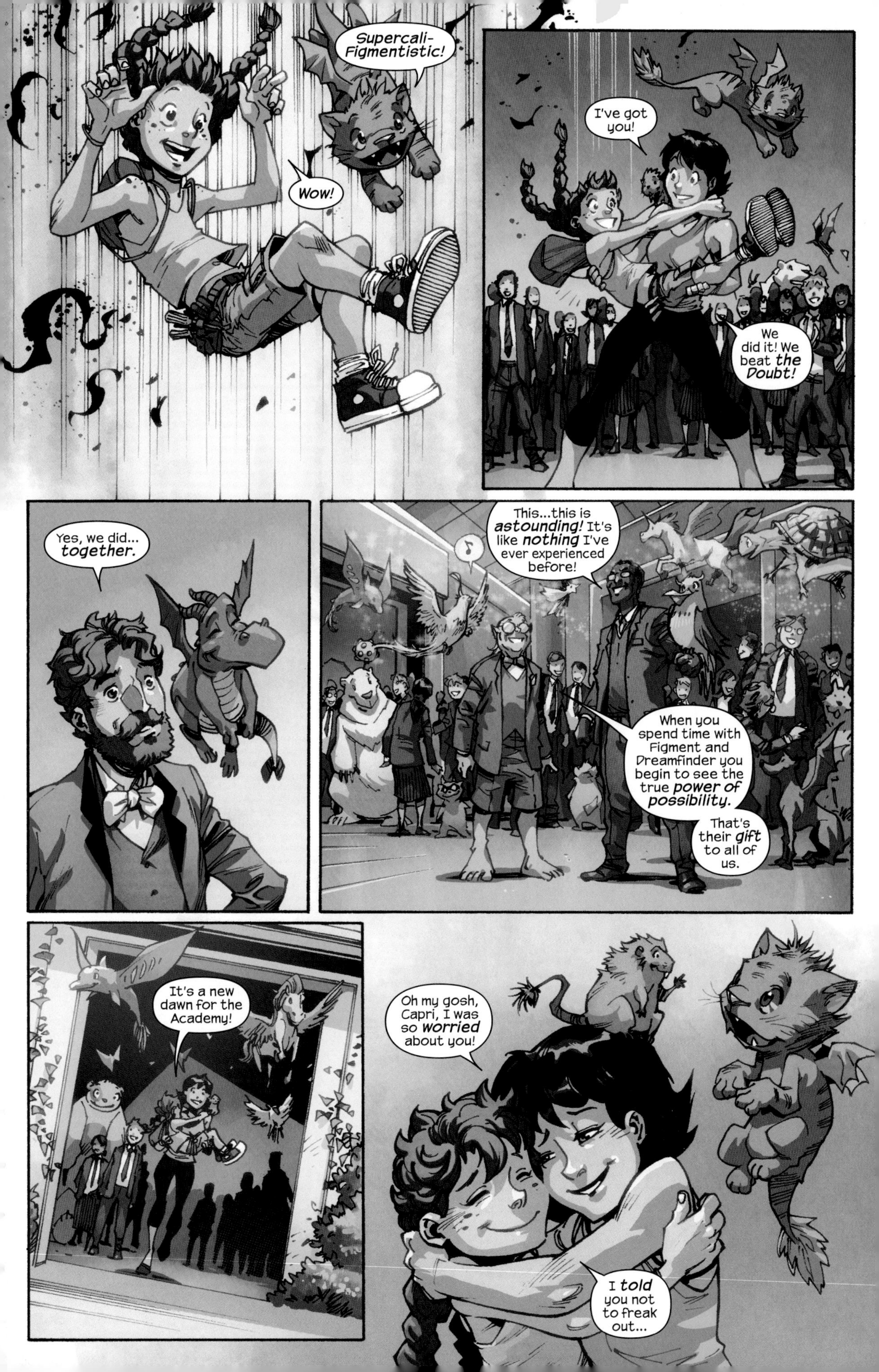
Supercali-Figmentistic!
Wow!
I've got you!
We did it! We beat the Doubt!
Yes, we did... together.
This...this is astounding! It's like nothing I've ever experienced before!
♪
When you spend time with Figment and Dreamfinder you begin to see the true power of possibility.
That's their gift to all of us.
It's a new dawn for the Academy!
Oh my gosh, Capri, I was so worried about you!
I told you not to freak out...

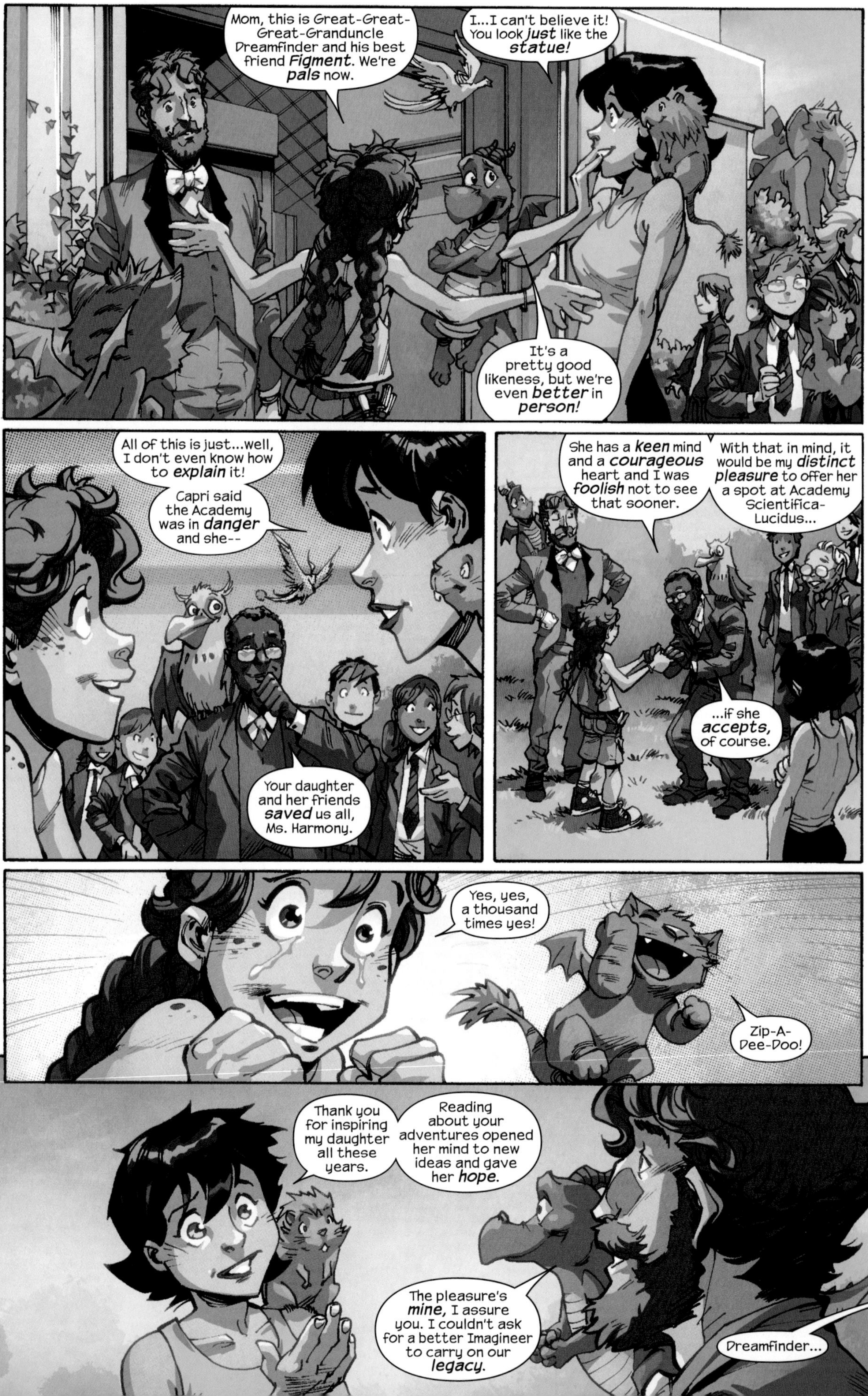
Mom, this is Great-Great-Great-Granduncle Dreamfinder and his best friend *Figment*. We're *pals* now.
I...I can't believe it! You look *just* like the *statue!*
It's a pretty good likeness, but we're even *better* in *person!*
All of this is just...well, I don't even know how to *explain* it!
Capri said the Academy was in *danger* and she--
Your daughter and her friends *saved* us all, Ms. Harmony.
She has a *keen* mind and a *courageous* heart and I was *foolish* not to see that sooner.
With that in mind, it would be my *distinct pleasure* to offer her a spot at Academy Scientifica-Lucidus...
...if she *accepts,* of course.
Yes, yes, a thousand times yes!
Zip-A-Dee-Doo!
Thank you for inspiring my daughter all these years.
Reading about your adventures opened her mind to new ideas and gave her *hope*.
The pleasure's *mine,* I assure you. I couldn't ask for a better Imagineer to carry on our *legacy*.
Dreamfinder...

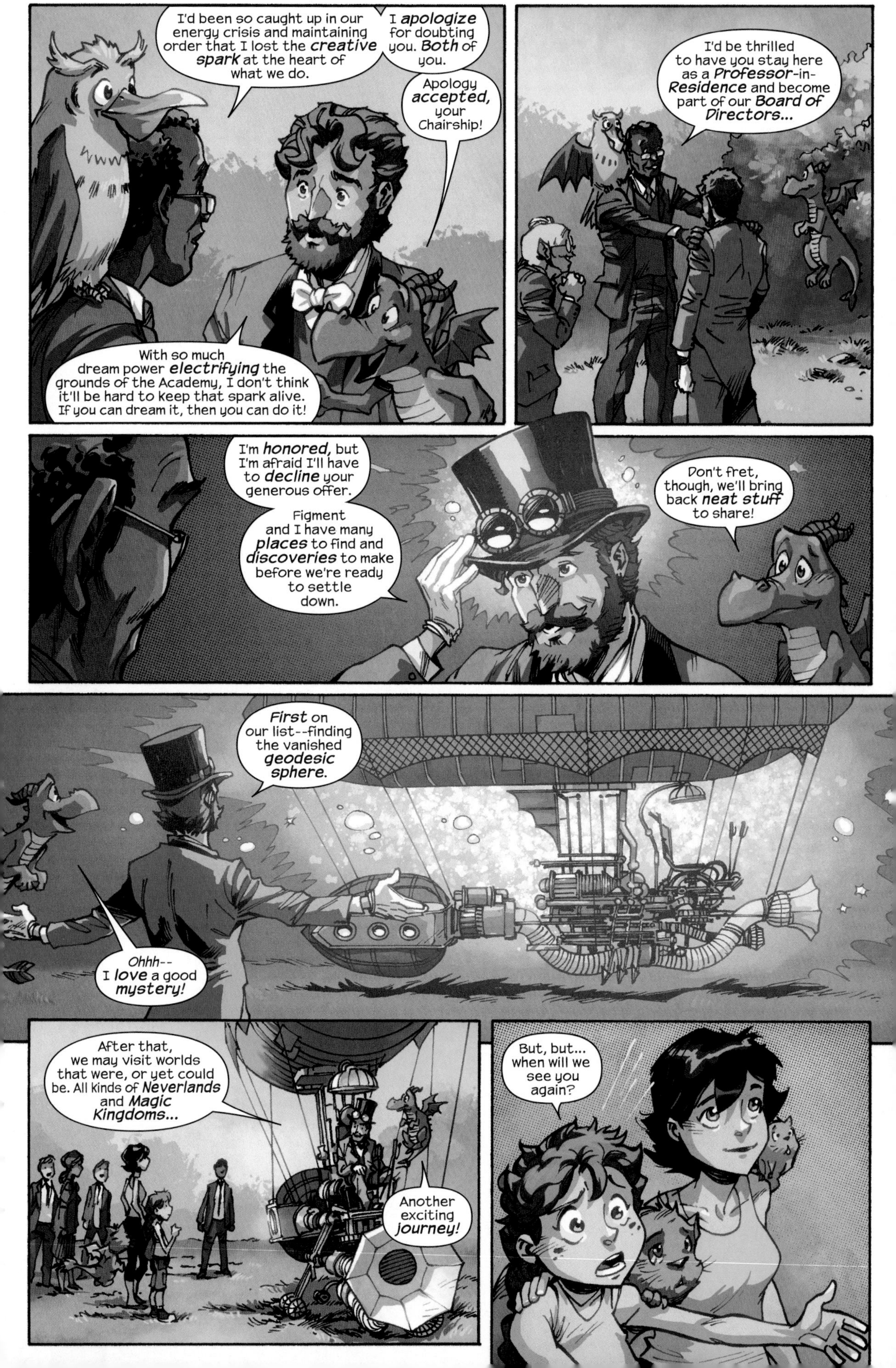

I'd been so caught up in our energy crisis and maintaining order that I lost the *creative spark* at the heart of what we do.
I *apologize* for doubting you. *Both* of you.
Apology *accepted,* your Chairship!
With so much dream power *electrifying* the grounds of the Academy, I don't think it'll be hard to keep that spark alive. If you can dream it, then you can do it!
I'd be thrilled to have you stay here as a *Professor*-in-*Residence* and become part of our *Board of Directors...*
I'm *honored,* but I'm afraid I'll have to *decline* your generous offer.
Figment and I have many *places* to find and *discoveries* to make before we're ready to settle down.
Don't fret, though, we'll bring back *neat stuff* to share!
First on our list--finding the vanished *geodesic sphere.*
Ohhh-- I *love* a good *mystery!*
After that, we may visit worlds that were, or yet could be. All kinds of *Neverlands* and *Magic Kingdoms...*
Another exciting *journey!*
But, but... when will we see you again?

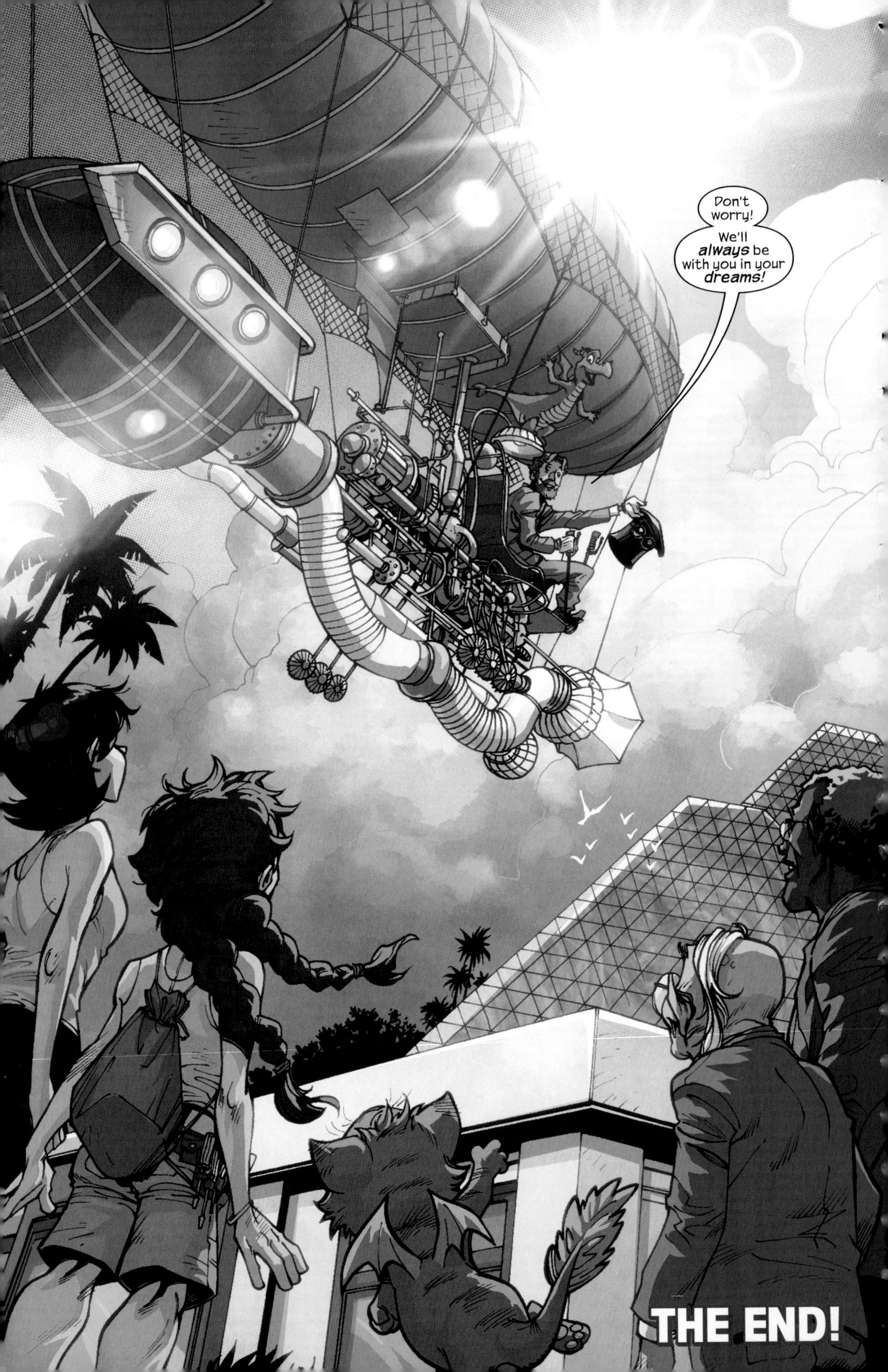
Don't worry! We'll always be with you in your dreams!
THE END!